My Biographies

Dreams and visions

By J Perez.

Intro:

 Contact ships begin from other worlds at 13 years of age1973.

has its biography: at Boy.
biography My Dreams and visions Realtime J Perez

was born in Santa Isabel village south of Puerto Rico humble cradle, with dreams of overcoming. With the ability to break down the limits of the imposed borders of free thought, it aspires to a better quality of life for human beings with respect for nature and all living beings. He has the firm conviction that he has been chosen to bring a message of peace to humanity and to be able to illuminate the entire galaxy with his light, of course with the help of many others like him and the blessing of the almighty.

As a Young Man,

His life has been colored by a number of experiences, events, dreams, premonitions that even without putting on paper haunted his mind as he had not fully fulfilled the purpose he had been assigned. His way of believing in an omnipresent God, different from the one everyone acclaims, reaffirms his line of thought and inspires him to unveil or decipher each message to share it with the world.

From Duato

Mas now as an adult at 57 years old, j Pérez's desire to raise awareness in the world with his stories and stories between real and fiction, trying to fulfill more than one dream, find the true origin of life and death, and create a balance of life between him and the humanity that surrounds him thus carrying a message of peace and love with the favor of the creator.

My life since I was a child has been full of nuances. From stories received without knowing what they wanted to say or what they meant for my life. My first contact with something strange was when I was 5 years old, they lifted me up in front of a deceased friend and when I looked inside I saw how he opened his eyes and from that moment I had panic and amazement at all that were the dead; when he was 10 years old; when I went through rivers or lakes or some place with a lot of water I panicked, I felt that something was pulling me and that it was going to take me away; However, at the age of 12 and as the years went by, I had many changes that would make me see life differently. So today, I can be more comfortable being someone special to my creator; When I was 13 years old, I had my first close encounter with some kind of strange being, which is not until today that I am an adult I can understand everything; so when i was sleeping i had my first case something sat on my bed while i slept but i felt the weight when under the mature and it was an old mature of fluff from the eternal rubber and when i felt that i didn't see anyone and I wouldn't know how It was possible, I got wet on myself and started calling my uncle scared, even today I still don't know for sure if he was a spiritual being; at that moment everything was spinning, my uncle told me and I am sure it was, after that moment I became afraid of the dark, I did not want to sleep in the dark which is already fearful; Well, a year went by, after the first strange event, a curious monk came to my house dressed as from the time of Jesus, a brown robe, he came from a direct alley, and my mother and he were talking, she gave him food and to take. Then he left, he disappeared on the same road behind some reed beds. In those days I didn't pay much attention to him, only now an adult and he asked me what was a person doing in the 70s dressed like this in Puerto Rico? Curious. The next event occurred months later, when I was at my grandfather's house; I had direct visual contact with three unidentified ships, as it was not possible in 1973 for something like exist for the eyes of a Puerto Rican, that night around 7 pm or 8 pm it was getting dark, and my grandfather was together with my grandmother and my mother. He had come to pick me up that afternoon that day, my grandfather used to play dominoes with my grandmother and I, and we had already finished and I was leaving with my mother and at that moment Papa Luis calls me from the boat and my grandmother and my mother and we He says look over the hills behind the school at the top there were astonishingly three space ships said Dad Luis, my grandfather said Lola look at that and when they moved a little more to the hill it was about 15 minutes we went out to the street to see Better to close the fence of the piece of cane when suddenly the ships were three with colored lights giving flashing beads very beautiful in themselves silver, with a speed that is not explainable, from the hill they went at lightning speed to the side From the south of my town you could see it from my grandfather's house, the view was in one piece, we watched as an island called the box of the dead landed on top and suddenly they turned three times and the ships left confused as if they were submerged in the water, then a straight line from above the island was turned three times and a direct line to the stars. The event was very impressive, they disappeared into the stars and scared we only commented that it would be that; For those years it was not so surprising, we took it as something happened normal according to my grandfather, as if a meteorite fell or some star moved and so it was that day, my mother took me home but today I study everything as if it had been in The moment he saw the ships I recess that moment but I was not the only one, my grandfather, my grandmother and my mother saw it, I think my grandfather had lived it before he worked since dawn in the cane fields so he could see the starry sky all the time dawn and he just laughed as if he had lived it before. Years later I learned that my mother and brothers saw behind.

another hill but he no longer lived in Puerto Rico; so the weeks went by and; Another strange event came into my life when I was 13 years old again was when we were about to sleep in an old zinc and poor wood house we felt a big blow something fell on the zinc from above a high house, nobody could climb and kept jumping Hard knocks for about 10 minutes through a window I had a sink in the air, my mother ran to close it and then put my brother between two pieces of wood on the wall and then after a while my grandfather arrived, scared we still did not go out my grandfather with a machete very quickly, he ran through the courtyard as if he knew what it was and he asked me today how did he find out? How did it get there so fast if you lived like a mile down in the neighborhood? the next day the neighbor closest to the house told my mother what fell on the zinc was a winged animal similar to a gargoyle and; Once again I think today if it is related to the sighting or he wanted to scare us or he had bad intentions because every day stranger things happened, I decided to learn about the stars, I wanted to be a parapsychologist and asked for courses; later in the month I had a problem at home and my mother beat me up I ran barefoot with shorts, torn dirty shirt, running in the middle of neighborhoods, I crossed a river, a mountain, it was like 5 in the afternoon I was not there dark but later it got dark a bit, I crossed the river of another neighboring town called Juana Diaz I arrived near a military base, the funny thing was that I crossed all that in a short time, running without spitting a single thorn, or cutting myself a little, just I was running in terror as if I had been frightened; I came to a short cane field on the side of the military base and the road; I thought I would go where an aunt in Ponce, another town, after

Juana Diaz made me sleepy, scared, I threw myself between the gray hairs, on a fence until I fell asleep and I don't know what happened, no animal bit me, nothing came near me, I was afraid to the darkness, the dead; That night, I was brave as if it were not me, the next day I woke up and started on my way to my aunt's house, it was strange, I arrived the first time without Later I dreamed of a reptilian woman, the funny thing was that she said she was my mother and she showed me how in a past life in a world with a platform of crystals to control a time portal and she told me this piece of gold and a scroll, bury it here that I remembered; In another dream, I dreamed of a code, the most curious and the most relevant, I dreamed 1.11 that number, from that day I see it everywhere but all, hours, letters, post on my website, everything, cards, codes, even in some pairs years later I discovered it was my main purpose I got it in,

 Revelation 1:11 that said: Write in a book what you see, and ...

bibliaparalela.com ›revelation› 1-11

Revelation 1: 8,17 I am the Alpha and the Omega - says the Lord God - the What is and what was and what is to come, the Almighty… What. Revelation 1:19 Write then what you have seen, and what are, and what will happen after them. Revelation 2: 1

I did the same in 2019, I wrote my first book called Portal code RHN-G portal, what I saw, the angel, they gave me the code of my purpose, RHN, means RH Negative special blood which can be a brother from space or a being divine including Jesus Christ, I tried to interpret dreams as I could, that is, the greatest thing is not everything I tell you, it is that every time I dream something special since I started writing dreams. Days, months, and years go by, a prophetic message arrived, I do not feel that I am not at prophet, I just transmit a message to the world that should know, but it is hard to transmit the truth, the world likes lies, darkness, and power; when a good being wants to carry a message it becomes impossible, but faith, truth, and my free will is stronger. In each written book, I carry a story taken from my dreams, messages, visions, not only do I tell the story but I create it in fiction so that the reader is entertained and can receive the message without transferring, if I tell him directly he would be scared, like this that when I say the dream or the message and it happens, they think that this is my technique. My mission, so far, I have written 6 books; Each book has many dreams inside it, but my last two this.

year are the most forceful and clear as I tell you.

1- 23 May 2019

Strange
dream of A new dream strange and prophetic vision, that's what I saw. a number of people running to get on airplanes, leaving an island because someone said in a very loud voice that a volcano would erupt in 5 hours, it could be five hours, 5 days but since they left five it was very early and I was looking for my loved ones and I think my time is running out, this would end and the island would sink due to the eruption. What is true in that? as all people do not care they never believe until they see so I did run to look for my relatives, now where will it be? On which island? and in my mind I said, my God let me save my loved ones so watch out for a volcano disappearing an island in about five days, who knows 5 weeks, let's hope they will be better in 5 thousand years.

2-8 May 2021

dream vision with fighter jets in a populated space.

Good morning, I had a vision, I dream this day because it is 11:30 AM and I woke up with a terrifying dream that I never want to happen but it is the first of its kind, I woke up from an attack between warplanes and; The only thing I heard after seeing the terrifying scene are those from India, we ran looking for a refuge where we could cover ourselves with the pieces of planes and pieces of pieces of burning bone, no idea but looking up at the sky hundreds of planes were seen on fire crossed like madness attacks from side to side, it is imminent I said to myself that they attack us it would be possible that today Saturday 8/5/21 hours a message is seen through a dreamlike vision, the place I saw was between a neighborhood of Puerto Rico and then I saw myself as a neighborhood In hills like the favelas of Brazil there are some poor scenarios there I saw that the attack could be a poor country, but it was a kind of war because there were many planes attacking, without stones I took refuge in a business with a wooden roof, because it seemed very dangerous to me I was already running out of strength and when I saw a parachute fall from fright I woke up regretful about this pole, but it felt so real that I am still in shock but it is also to warn and I know r CAREFUL, EYE always up, we are in difficult times, everything can happen, God protect you all, it is not a story from my books, it was a horrible vision in my dreams.

More the piece of rocket that had to fall from China fell into the Indian Sea as well as the dream says two things in the same dream.

This dream vision came out 2 days after the Palestinian attack on Israel and Gaza.

3- I dream of the vision of the ships in the forest of the anvil

Dream vision around the 10th to the 11th of May I had a very strange vision in which I was walking in a forest with a brother like that I told him, I think he was a brother from the church where I was from Years ago but, He was driving in the forest in a jeep. There was a mountain in the woods. He said that I had a mission to fulfill. I tell him ok if we go, it seemed strange to me that he said this to me being a brother of the church; more we continue a few miles further into the hill and we descend at the end of the road there he told me enter there behind those weeds and you will see your destination then I said ok thank you and he left and left me there, I walked inside the mountain towards the point la hill full of vegetation and to my surprise I found a kind of entrance inside a ship and very excited I had memories of the past when I saw a similar one in my years as a child, I walked without fear since in my visions I am not afraid, I feel protected, there I heard a voice that told me come, without fear we wait for you, and I saw how a scientist woman with silver clothes and tall, of Nordic race, but without hair, big eyes of strange color, but similar to us ok I said I continued inside, I They said here you are, you see here is full of animals, In the ship this is what we do here is to collect animals to fill a new world that the creators have almost ready for your race in years to come, I asked and what am I doing here? We wanted to teach you, you saw us years ago as a child and you have always wondered what we were doing even though you never said something or didn't tell someone what happened, your family and you deserved to know they were very faithful and kept quiet. And I answered her, yes of course if I speak they would also call me crazy or something like that, and she continued talking: well these animals are the new generation, we look for samples and we seek to make our purpose and now we will take a little trip with you here was this ship for Years and that The suitcase that you brought that the man who brought you had had a part of the old ship that was lost for thousands of Years was here all the time waiting for you to continue the journey and transport the specimens between blood samples and plant samples that we need in the new world, and suddenly the ship flew off I felt that when I walked on its nickel or titanium metal floor, I can still feel it, it still sounded like stepping on a piece of aluminum or titanium metal, which made me hold on tight with fright; the ship flew suddenly something jumped to the ground it was a kind of fish similar to those from Japan that had a spirituality I thought but the scientist said it out loud, I said the same. How did you hear me? Then she said we can read your mind, your thought, we have always accompanied you from afar, and you have just saved the goldfish specimen, it is one of the few that still exist, it is a Japanese koi with a lot of energy and brings a lot of peace, it is A spiritual fish is many years old you cannot imagine how long it is here inside this ship waiting for this moment and we will take it to its final destination a new world, just because of the bad treatment of some powerful, they made us crash years ago we lost a part of the ship, how sad and that part is what makes the ship take flight and destiny with that we fly. Do you know what is inside I said what is it? Could you at least know? Yes, of course, she said and answered my question: it is a special crystal that the ship that crashed had, we got it with beings that they do not even know how to use it, some very skilled beings helped us to bring them from a laboratory; for them it was a colored stone. However, you have already seen them in dreams, previous visions, you remember your mother from the past, the good reptilian in the green pyramids that she gave you and that she told you about some crystalline stones, so I replied: ah how so really? If she gave me a piece of gold and a parchment, we found out together and she showed me a base as a control panel with several stones, and the woman continued talking: yes of course that was the control panel of our ships, open a teleporter, and that's how it was as well we go out in other worlds fast and the parchment what is it? I asked, and she replied: they are the coordinates of your world, she had it saved, and the gold was the payment for another being that she will collect there to bring to us. All a kind of mission, everything is linked georky today they tell you the truth and we already fulfilled, you fulfilled although you still have a lot of work to do, now tell your story and take this your first relics of the past is in this little box, when you recover them all now They can do another mission, I took it and left the ship; then they brought me back after a ride so I could feel what flying saucer rides were like. Then, I went into the forest and the friend was already there waiting for me and we left after a happy moment, I woke up not before remembering the whole vision, I have a secret of how I forget everything except the vision that I will tell you in another chance. I woke up, waited several minutes and when I was ready, I opened my eyes and began to write what I dreamed of and everything I saw, I did not put it in my networks. this time it was direct here, for my book of the relics of the past.

Check in Geo.
https://www.facebook.com/geo.ejecutador/
https://twitter.com/Ejecutador31
Where I post all my dreams

And another that I went into a story the last dream days ago has to do with an astral dream, I had my first before understanding what astral dreams were because I knew it because I still feel when I took the steps in the ships inside where they let me enter my dreams back I felt them accompanied the incredible iron I say it and as if it were right there, message on a new world created by him created for the future.

Here the dreams posted on twitter with their days and years, check if any of them fall as I say until the black gold book, I said before that book will pass, only the rain of fire has not happened, the rest has been happening little by little.
Here
Post dreams real visions I had on various days post on Facebook or twitter which I also adapted in books as Divine messages.

J Perez
@ GeoPleyadiano30
·Sep 16, 2019
IMMINENT RISE OF PETROLEÓ 09/15/2019, in my book, is the prophecy gathering and The World did not pay attention to me, Luego Sera trade writes be prophesy in my book two months ago since some history of my book, Now is True.
https://read.amazon.com/kp/embed?asin=B07W55WSQW & preview = newtab & linkCode = kpe & ref_ = cm_sw_r_kb_dp_DY8FDb6WJDF05 & tag = geoperez-20

J Perez

@ GeoPleyadiano30

·Apr 20, 2019

Dream visions were people in an open place and at the moment an attack with airplanes dropping explosive objects that annihilated the adjacent people and ran to hide us in underground places so I saw it. amazon.com/jorge-perez/e/ B07LCVJJ5S ref = dbs_p_ebk_r00_abau_000000 ... ... #bookadaptation #game of Thrones

J Perez

@ GeoPleyadiano30

·April 20, 2019

Dream Prophetic Vision, in my vision I saw a beach full of people on a beautiful day and apparently deep in the sea a giant tremor made the either go back and there was a terrifying tsunami but I saw people running scared. amazon.com/jorge-perez/e/ B07LCVJJ5S ref = dbs_p_ebk_r00_abau_000000 ... #bookadaptation #gameofthrones

J Perez

@ GeoPleyadiano30

·Mar 28, 2019

Dream, Prophetic Vision Platform As a mother ship-shaped in the form of a platform, it flew in orbit nearby, to planet, rounding it up, dreaming Leave us some other HAD HAD Already day and repeated the message Real Life #bookadaptation #booktofilm #adaptation #authors

J Perez

@ GeoPleyadiano30

·Mar 28, 2019

Prophetic Dream Vision VI as a mothership inform
of Platform flying in orbit around the planet still
dream round Quit vu had any other day and
repeated message O prophecia Real Life
#bookadaptation #booktofilm #adaptation #authors

J Perez
@ GeoPleyadiano30

·Mar 20, 2019
Early Morning Dream Wednesday, March 20/2019
Dream of launched projectiles and a directed
drone ready to launch with a dangerous projectile,
the dream happened similar dream and as vision
or message I already have. https:
.facebook.com/geo.ejecutador
J Perez
@ GeoPleyadiano30

·Mar 18, 2019
Dream, Vision, Prophecy. The Pope while visiting
a country I saw as a priest under his robes, I had a

**weapon with a silencer and as I saw, I felt a
very real dream of my life. I did not ask to hear
it come. #PortalCodeRHNGSuenosPropheticos.
J Perez**
@GeoPleyadiano30

·Oct 31, 2018
**PortalCoDeRHN-G -Dream Prophecies Ring
Solomon Changed at the time of his death and
melted Where is in code discover him and
Many more secrets unveiled in dreams and
who controls it, The fall of a modern empire in
series of books soon #HappyHalloween
J Perez**

·Oct 31, 2018
PortalCoDeRHN-G -Dream Prophecies Ring Solomon Changed at the time of his death and melted Where is in code discover him and Many more secrets unveiled in dreams and who controls it, The fall of a modern empire in series of books soon #HappyHalloween
J Perez

weapon with silencer and as I saw, I felt a very real dream of my life. I did not ask to hear it coming.
#PortalCodigoRHNGSuenosPropheticos.
J Perez

·October 31, 2018
PortalCoDeRHN-G -Dream Prophecies Ring Solomon changed at the time of his death and melted Where is code and find out many more secrets unveiled in dreams and who controls, the fall of a modern empire book series soon #HappyHalloween
J Perez

·October 31, 2018
PortalCoDeRHN-G -Dream Prophecies Ring Solomon changed at the time of his death and melted Where is code and find out many more secrets disclosed in dreams and who controls, the fall of an empire modern in book series soon #HappyHalloween

J Perez
 @ GeoPleyadiano30

·September 29, 2018
http://poltalcoderhn-g.orgprophetic Eye Messages in dreams something that falls in the Caribbean See it in the link Very shocking and Real Dream Divine messages must Believe them #World citizen

J Perez
 @ GeoPleyadiano30

·September 25, 2018
https://poltalcoderhn-g.org
1
J Perez
 @ GeoPleyadiano30

·September 24, 2018
http://poltalcodigorhn-g.org eye Messages in dreams Something prophetic that falls in the Caribbean see it in the link very shocking and Real dream the divine messages must Believe them #BeAVoter
J Perez
 @ GeoPleyadiano30

·Sep 24, 2018
http://poltalcodigorhn-g.orgprophetic Eye Messages in dreams something that falls in the Caribbean See it in the link Very shocking and Real Dream Divine messages must Believe them #BeAVoter
J Perez
 @ GeoPleyadiano30

·Sep 24, 2018
http:// **poltalcodigorhn-g.orgprophetic Eye Messages in dreams something that falls in the Caribbean See it in the link Very shocking and Real Dream Divine messages must Believe them #DreamproPheciesEYESON**
J Perez
@ GeoPleyadiano30

·Sep 24, 2018
http:// **poltalcodigorhn-g.org eye Prophetic Messages in dreams something that falls in the Caribbean seeing the very shocking and actual link Dream divine messages should be Believe it #DreamproPheciesEYESON**
J Perez
@ GeoPleyadiano30

·November 12, 2017
Dreams or prophecies History geo spiritual contact 49 years in silence more tactile messages preferences preference UFO 1973

J Perez
@ GeoPleyadiano30
·October 16, 2017
Soldiers PR, USA, they don't need us but we fight in the front row free pr

Geo Executor
September 16, 2019 ·

IMMINENT RISE OF OIL 09/15/2019, in my book is the prophecy Fulfilling and The World did not pay attention to me Then it will be late I wrote that prophecy in my book two months ago since I dreamed the story of my book Now it became reality. https://read.amazon.com/kp/embed…

INMINENT RISE OF PETROLEÓ 09/15/2019, in my book, it is the gathered prophecy, and the world did not pay attention to me. months since a bit of history from my book, Now is True. https://read.amazon.com/kp/embed ...

Shared via Kindle. Description: This story begins in mid-2019 between Jordan and Dubai, in a city of families who owned the oil empire, they were studied and prepared for the Saif Al Karak world. A Jordanian son of Muhannad Al Karak, owner of almost all Jordanians ...
READ.AMAZON.COM

Saif Al Karak's Legacy: Black Gold (Short Story V1)

Shared via Kindle. Description: This story begins in

mid-2019 between Jordan and Dubai, in a city of

families who owned the oil empire, they were studied

and prepared for the Saif Al Karak world. A Jordanian

son of Muhannad Al Karak, owner of almost all

Jordanians ...

Shared via Kindle. Description: This story begins in mid-2019 between Jordan and Dubai, in a city of families who owned the oil empire, they were studied and prepared for the Saif Al Karak world. A Jordanian son of Muhannad Al Karak, owner of almost all Jordanians ...

2 comments 1 share

Comments
See one more comment

-
- **Geo Ejecutadorr** there is the proof that my book is a sign that it is happening today exactly as it is written in my book, the oil rises and brings conflict so Those who believed in me see it in MY book because they got it Those who did not nothing to read written

more than 5 months ago and today the unexpected happens reflect and look for the creator. . https://read.amazon.com/kp/embed? asin = B07WZV92NR ...

Geo Executor

August 8, 2019 ·

They continue to ignore the messages that God sends us through Privileged beings of Light, I confess Child I have been able to see and perceive things in dreams, so everything happens according to what They are the plans of the creator and something much greater is coming. A great civil uprising that will bring many peoples to their knees to pray, before a disastrous outbreak of tremors and volcanoes simultaneously erupting, an inevitable fact, it is too late. Without counting the rain of fire, nature itself will warn us of the moment, let's not attack ourselves but join in a single force and the greatest thing about the time of invasions I saw in three different dreams in the middle of a war invasions of ships of Other worlds or would it be getting involved in the lawsuit for or against something big is about eye everything is written and said nothing more than to tell they know what to do.

This prophecy, I hope you remember that I have been predicting a dream that I had and what would happen today, I have seen how something that is happening is happening in New Jersey, with a string of tornadoes in a city that has never arisen before and that is happening.

Quote a tweet.

J Perez

@ GeoPleyadiano30

· June 11

The vision of the dream prophecy with Deja vu is real, it is repeated 3 times and it is a very real

eminent tornado chain that enters where hurricanes and great devastations have never been seen before. May God take care of us. It is a true dream, message, and understatement. #TuesdayThoughts #taleflick
This prophecy, I hope you remember that I have been predicting a dream that I had and what would happen today I have seen as something that is happening is happening in New Jersey, with a string of tornadoes in a city that had never happened before. He was resurrected and that is happening.
Quote Tweet
J Perez
@ GeoPleyadiano30
· June 11
Prophecy Vision dreams Deja Vu real, repeated 3 times and it is an eminent chain of tornadoes Very real, entering hurricanes and great devastations have never been seen before. May God take care of us. It's a real dream, message, and understatement. Tuesday #taleflick
Geo Executioner

May 23, 2019 ·

A Dream strange
dream a strange new and prophetic vision, behold I saw a number of people getting on planes running and out of an island because someone said a voice very struendo a volcano Aryan eruption in 5 it could be five hours 5 days but since five came out, it was very early and I was looking for my loved ones among the people and I think my time was running out, this would end and the island would sink because of the eruption, what is true in that ? As all people do not care they never believe until they see so I did run to look for my relatives, now where will it be? On what island? and in my mind I said my God let me save my loved ones so watch out for a volcano disappearing in about five days. Who

knows, in 5 weeks let's hope that 5 thousand years better be like that.

A new dream, a strange and prophetic vision, I saw several people running in planes leaving an island because someone said in a very loud voice that an Aryan volcano in 5 can be five hours 5 days but since five came out they were very early and I was looking to my loved ones among the people and I think that time was running out this would end and the island would sink from the eruption which is true of that, as all the people do not care, they never believe until they see me. Yes, I ran to find my relatives now where will it be on which island and in my mind, it said: OMG, let me save my loved ones, so face to face with a volcano that disappears on an island in about five days, who knows, 5 weeks I hope a thousand years better this way.

do not underestimate dreams.

June 11, 2019
 Dream Astral vision.

Prophecy Vision dreams Deja Vu real, repeats 3 times and is a very real eminent, a chain of Tornadoes entering where hurricanes and great devastation have never been seen before. May God take care of us. It is a true dream, message, and understatement.

Prophecy Dreams of Vision Dejavu real, repeated 3 times and it is an eminent Very real, chain of Tornadoes entering where Hurricanes and great devastations have never been seen before. May God take care of us. It is a true dream, message, and understatement ... today they are going out of control of the climate.

There is this post on Facebook before everything about the fallen rocket and the attacks from the Middle East and others happened, that is, my dream, vision was days before and boom. The unexpected happened.

Geo ejecutador

.

Shared with: Public.

Dream vision outbreak with war planes in a populated space.
Good morning I had a dream vision this day because it is 11:30 AM and I woke up with a terrifying dream that I never want to happen but it is the first of its kind, I woke up from an attack between warplanes and the only thing I heard after seeing the terrifying scenario was in India, I was running looking for a refuge where to cover myself from the pieces of planes and pieces of lit pieces that is, I have no idea but looking up from the sky there were hundreds of planes in crossfire like a crazy thing attacks from the side winged is eminent I said to myself they attack us it would be possible

that today Saturday 5/8/21 hour 5/8/21 a message is seen through a dream vision, the place was seen to be between a neighborhood of Puerto Rico and then I saw myself as a neighborhood in hills like the favelas of Brazil, some poor scenery, there, I saw the attack, it could be a poor country, but it was a kind of war, because there were many planes attacking without stones, I took refuge in a business with a wooden roof, because it seemed very dangerous already I Or what was falling outside and when I saw a parachute falling from the scare awake, sorry for this post but it felt so real that I was still in shock but it is not enough to warn and be careful EYE We are always up in difficult times everything can happen God protect you to all . It is not the history of my books, it was a horrible vision in my dreams, vision, the place I saw was between a neighborhood in Puerto Rico and then I saw myself as a neighborhood in hills like the favelas of Brazil some poor scenario there I saw the attack could be A poor country but it was a kind of war because there were many planes attacking without stones I took refuge in a business with a wooden roof because it seemed very dangerous and what was falling outside and when I saw parachutes falling from the scare I woke up sorry for this post but it felt so real

that I am still in shock but it is not
enough to warn and be careful Be careful
always up we are in difficult times
everything can happen God protect you
all. Constar is not the history of my
books. It was a horrible vision in my
dreams.

I had a sighting for several hours at half an hour
then it disappeared here I send you the photos.
a strange object on the right side of the moon a
little below. I leave it to your discretion I have
investigated.

J perez NAME OF THE BOOKS

PortalCodeRHN-G

Code Portal RHN-G2

Port Code RHN-G3
The Millennial Secret of Sam Stewart, a time traveler
Saif Al Karak's legacy: Black Gold

Georky

The Seventh Relic of the Lost Treasure

Create the trilogy: code portal RHN-G the trilogy

Nowadays I am writing about my Biography, each book has its Audible for blind people. For now, in English version.

So JPerez has an idea, I will be writing until the world finds the reason for my messages is not for money but the duty of a son, of a creator to whom we owe the life that the creator has given us, bless you today tomorrow and always remember to santify Ask for

forgiveness from the creator and your neighbor, also forgive and forget everything from scratch; They will have their minds, free yourselves from the slavery of a system, we are in the world but we are not of the world and we have never been alone. It is the purpose, help me to take it and there is more but it will be another time, thank you.

Creator's message for today 11/5/2021

Future:

comes something much bigger something that there will be no place to hide if you do not prepare better and will enter directly from another world parallel to this as a dimensional change the adjustment of the planet is in process since the 70s "I have felt it but I had not understood it , the birds the animals go crazy and things around are changing we will enter a dimensional process because bad energies enter from another dimensional zone only to take over; we must create the opposite to

create good energies to counteract as a war
between parallel worlds close the door
Beings of light cannot fight alone, we must
give them faith, strength, belief, as well as
evil has gained strength through a diverse
group of followers, the light needs us and
we, united, will create the energy force to
return to what we were before creating a
wall between parallel worlds by faith, the
hope of what is not seen, the certainty of
what is not expected everything that's the
truth.

Wake up we have been used for millennia by
dark beings for the simple fact of being calm
humans have made us hostile, aggressive to
everything, irrational, even our families we do not
distinguish as long as we do what is convenient for
us the method of enslaving ourselves now in The
system has made us forget our roots, we need
them to wake up and think from the deepest
memories as we were in the past and fear the
creator, respect the laws of the creator, the true
ones, not those that man has created by power or
convenience, there will be Concentrate your
minds, close your eyes to evil and see your inner
light that will provide you with divine energies
according to your faith, santify yourselves and you
will obtain the change, the key to success, visualize
your good memories, happy to fight the bad ones,
use nature It is the most logical thing to establish

our level in the spiritual, nature gives us peace and love.

We have never been alone.

By JPerez.

Audibles JPerez.

https://www.audible.com/pd/Portal-Code-RHN-G-Audiobook/B091FWMCYF?asin=B091FWMCYF

Please enjoy one free audio review copy of Portal Code RHN-G (PortalcodeRHN-G 1 Trilogy Dreams Prophecies Visions), now available on Audible. Redeem the one-time use code below at https://www.audible.co.uk/acx-promo.

Code

2QFZAE55R7EHL

https://www.audible.com/search?keywords=portal+code+RHN-G3&ref=a_pd_The-Mi_t1_header_search

Please enjoy one free audio review copy of Portal Code RHN-G3: GF The heroes of the future Hunting the dark shadow (PortalCoDeRHN-G), now available on Audible. Redeem the one-time use code below at https://www.audible.com/acx-promo.

24RYWC3U4MDDW

---

https://www.audible.com/pd/The-Millennial-Secret-Sam-Stewarts-Travel-in-Time-Audiobook/B0931QHBX7?ref=a_typ_c1_lProduct_1&pf_rd_p=9161e73b-1da4-4835-9d0a-6e130501757a&pf_rd_r=BDEBKXRCM90YS2NXF4HR

Please enjoy one free audio review copy of Millennial Secret Sam Stewart's, Travel in Time: Travelers on time, now available on Audible. Redeem the one-time use code below at https://www.audible.com/acx-promo.

3382EE2XXEWGF

----

https://www.audible.com/search?keywords=The+legacy+of+Saif+Al+Karak%3A+Black+gold+%28short+story+V1%29&ref=a_pd_Portal_t1_header_search

Please enjoy one free audio review copy of the legacy of Saif Al Karak: Black gold (short story V1), now available on Audible. Redeem the one-time use code below at https://www.audible.com/acx-promo.

5S9FSEK8DBQB8

https://www.audible.com/pd/Cody-el-elfo-Y-la-varita-magica-Cody-the-Elf-and-the-Magic-Wand-Audiobook/B09HN5ZTY2?ref=a_library_t_c5_libItem_&pf_rd_p=80765e81-b10a-4f33-b1d3-ffb87793d047&pf_rd_r=1SVZES40JWFMCJ2Q4MET

By JPerez.